Araminta's Wedding

Araminta's Wedding

or
A Fortune Secured

A COUNTRY HOUSE EXTRAVAGANZA

pictures by
Sue Macartney-Snape
words by
Jilly Cooper

Mandarin

A Mandarin Paperback
ARAMINTA'S WEDDING

First published in Great Britain in 1993
by Methuen London
This edition published in 1994
by Mandarin Paperbacks
an imprint of Reed Consumer Books Ltd
Michelin House, 81 Fulham Road, London SW3 6RB
and Auckland, Melbourne, Singapore and Toronto

Pictures copyright © 1993 by Sue Macartney-Snape
Words copyright © 1993 by Jilly Cooper
The artist and author have asserted their moral rights

A CIP catalogue record for this book
is available at the British Library
ISBN 0 7493 1115 0

Designed by Katy Hepburn
Typeset by Intype, London
Printed in Great Britain by
BPC Hazell Books Ltd
A member of
The British Printing Company Ltd

Artist's Dedication

*To my mother
and in memory of my father*

Sue Macartney-Snape

Author's note

The pictures came first. They were brilliantly funny, often poignant, exquisitely observed, and teeming with splendid dogs. Utterly enchanted, hazily thinking of extended captions, I agreed to write a linking text.

After several failed attempts to write a series of little essays about English upper-class life (the only common tie between otherwise unrelated pictures) I resorted, in despair, to fiction. My problem was handling so many different characters. But at last I found a heroine in a schoolgirl hat (see page 52) and decided to call her Araminta. The fat slob in the same picture became her villainous cousin, Piggy, who, to my delight, I discovered playing bridge in another picture (page 20). Lounging in his bath, the epitome of caddish glamour (page 28), emerged my hero, Bounder Cartwright.

I only hope the end result complements Sue's gloriously idiosyncratic vision.

I would like to thank Rosie Abel-Smith and Andrew Parker-Bowles for reading early drafts and coming up with endless hilarious suggestions, and Annette Xuereb-Brennan for typing the manuscript.

I am also immensely grateful to Katy Hepburn for designing such a beautiful book and to Geoffrey Strachan and Mary O'Donovan for editing it. Geoffrey deserves particular gratitude for masterminding the entire operation and commuting between artist and author − not the easiest task − with such tact, humour and understanding.

Jilly Cooper

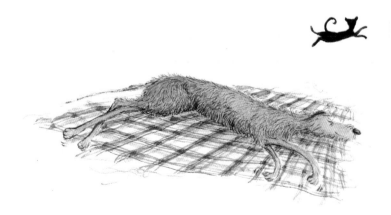

The Rousing of Rufus

1

On Boxing Night, Rufus, fifth Earl of Atherstone, slept with his fourth wife Rosebud for the first time in twenty years. This was entirely thanks to his eldest sister Pansy, who always got the wrong end of the stick. Believing the recently published Madonna book to be a learned treatise on paintings of the Virgin Mary, and hoping it might include the Titian Madonna which hung in the Great Hall at Flatgrove, Pansy ordered it for the Earl as a Christmas present. The consequences of this misunder-standing were far-reaching.

Earlier on Boxing Night, there had been a dinner party at Flatgrove. The food, which included pheasant shot by the Earl, was deliciously chilled because the maids had such a long trek from distant kitchens. The wines were infinitely worse than they should have been because Drinkwater, the butler, had already drunk the best.

Rufus Atherstone, who could trace his family back to William Rufus, had the same concussed air as his forebear of having been hit by a large branch. While his guests dis-cussed wife avoidance and tax avoidance and the latest demand for £250,000 from Lloyds, and wept crocodile tears over the even worse 'lorsses' of their friends, Rufus enjoyed a quiet sleep.

Peter Ponsonby-Porter, who was admired by his friends as 'a most amusing fellow', then invited the rest of the table to tell him who they would ask for directions if they were 'lorst' in the desert; a pink panther, an honest Lloyds broker, or a dishonest Lloyds broker?

The answer was the dishonest broker, because the other two were figments of the imagination. The helpless guffaws of laughter woke Rufus Atherstone, who had a second glass of port, and asked if anyone had heard news of Herbie Foxe-Whapshott's prostate.

'Poor fellow's in hospital with a cafeteria up his cock.'

2

Joining the Ladies

2

latgrove, the most beautiful house in Lincoln-shire, was seriously cold, the sort of place Eski-mos send their children to as punishment. Even the sleekest lurchers living there grew long shaggy coats. By the time the ladies had returned to the drawing-room from powdering their noses in distant bedrooms, the coffee was cold and Rufus's mistress, Flappy Foxe-Whapshott, who always behaved as though she owned the place, had hogged the fire. Drinkwater then offered the ladies a liqueur. They would have preferred kümmel. Unfortunately the kümmel was now inside Drinkwater, so they had to make do with armagnac.

Rufus's fourth wife Rosebud – with whom he had not slept since their honeymoon – was an excellent hostess, but unromantic. Once, when taken onto the terrace to admire the full moon, Rosebud had merely contemplated the silvery disc and pondered how many guests she could seat round it. Neither she nor Rufus could control Drinkwater.

Now was the time, rather than during dinner, for the other wives to compliment her on the delicious *moule* soufflé and how much Jean-Baptiste, the French chef, who'd formerly worked at the Dorchester, had blossomed. They then began peering surreptitiously inside the Christmas cards, most of which seemed to say: 'Jeremy was declared redundant in February, but Dommie got into Eton. Can't *think* where he gets his brains from!'

Knowing Rufus and their husbands would be at least an hour, everyone settled down to a serious bout of 'who's doing what to whom'. The discussion then moved on, as it always did, to Rufus's glamorous and wayward third wife, Grace, who had evidently just had her eyes done.

'Such agony, my dear, they peel the skin right orf your face,' said Flappy Foxe-Whapshott with relish. As Rufus's mistress of long standing, she detested Grace. 'That woman,' went on Flappy, 'has been pretending to people she's gone off to a health farm.'

'What's that?' quavered Rufus's sister Pansy, who had given him the Madonna book. 'Did you say Grace had run off with a healthy farmer?' Everyone thought this was 'frite-fly' funny.

By the time the men finally came out of the dining-room, it was half past ten, and Rufus Atherstone was yawning his head off and pointedly turning off lights. Mr Corker, the local wine merchant, who had only been asked because Rufus owed him so much money, was very put out. Having delivered so much drink to Flatgrove over the years, most of it admittedly consumed by Drinkwater, he and his wife had expected an evening of Bacchanalia and had ordered a minicab to collect them at midnight. They now had to creep down the drive and hover furtively by the main gate in the pouring rain and frantically flag down the minicab when it finally appeared.

Meanwhile, in a port-induced stupor, Rufus Atherstone had stumbled off to bed. Flipping through the Madonna book in search of the Flatgrove Titian, he was so turned on by the photographs of the knickerless pop star that he stumbled excitedly out onto the landing and instead of lurching right into Flappy Foxe-Whapshott's bedroom, turned left in confusion and jumped on an amazed Rosebud.

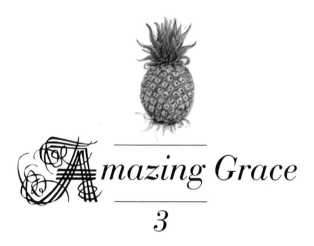

Amazing Grace

3

Rufus Atherstone had stopped making love to Rosebud, his fourth wife, on their honeymoon, because he realised that he was still hopelessly in love with his third wife, Grace. Grace had destroyed their marriage and broken his heart by eloping with his best friend, Peter Ponsonby-Porter, after giving birth to Rufus's only child, his daughter Araminta. Reluctant to relinquish her title, however, Grace had resisted marrying again.

Grace Atherstone, a great beauty, was nicknamed 'the Lincolnshire poacher' because, singing: 'It's my delight on a shining knight,' she had poached practically every husband in the county. Nor was it just Lincolnshire. Half the husbands in Knightsbridge, Kensington and Chelsea had done it with bad Grace.

The most fashionable woman of her age, she held court at Libertine Hall, ordering everyone around. Grace was also a setter of trends. The day she nonchalantly went to Ascot in a pair of black court shoes from which her new labrador puppy had eaten both toes, she started an instant fashion for peep-toed shoes, which was even adopted by the Royal Family.

Grace had terrific Ex-appeal and used huge dollops of charm to ride roughshod over people to get what she wanted. One Saturday night, when a young traffic cop had chased her home from a party at 100 mph, she had got off by batting her false eyelashes and sighing: 'Oh, I thought you were my friend, the Chief Constable, racing me home.'

Grace had always driven too fast. Friends had urged her to install sleeping policemen in her drive. But Grace preferred wide-awake policemen. The young traffic cop didn't get home until Monday.

For the last ten years, Grace had been supported by an Indian maharajah, whom she had bled almost white. But other swains were always hanging around: youths of great and insolent beauty.

And now their ranks had been joined by the ruby-faced

Joint Master of the Addlebury Hunt, Major Hiccup, who behaved even worse than Grace because he had a rich, ugly wife who refused to divorce him. Most of the marriages in Lincolnshire had suffered a Major Hiccup.

Hilda, the maid, was looking very boot-faced. Those dogs turned the bed into a gravel pit and the sheets had to be changed every day. And what's more, she hadn't been paid for three months. The Countess was constantly broke and forever threatening to sell her memoirs to the *Sunday Times*, a prospect which blanched even the florid cheeks of Major Hiccup.

Having abandoned Araminta as a tiny baby, Grace held her daughter in little affection. As she still only admitted to thirty-four, she didn't want a daughter of twenty hanging around.

For his part, having acrimoniously divorced Grace twenty years ago, Rufus Atherstone was still full of resentment and anguish. When he was in his cups, he hurled darts at her portrait, which still hung beside the Titian Madonna.

An illogical man, Rufus was better at taking issue than having it. Despite his refusal to sleep with Rosebud, he longed for a male heir to Flatgrove and the great estates in Lincolnshire and Wales that went with it. But all he had ever managed to produce after four marriages was Araminta, who would be worth a minta money on her twenty-first birthday when her trust fund matured, and even more when he died, but who could not inherit the title.

A Very Nice Girl

4

The daughter of a hundred Earls,
You are not one to be admired.

Tennyson

Lady Araminta Atherstone was not a beauty. When she patted you on the back she was liable to hurl you into the next county; but she was a very nice girl. Under that vast bosom, like ore hidden beneath a mountain, lurked a heart of gold. Having read somewhere that people grow to resemble their dogs, she had rescued a slender, elegant lurcher called Lightning, to whom she was utterly devoted. So far, however, her resemblance to Lightning remained scant.

Araminta was unofficially engaged to her cousin, Piggy Atherstone, who would inherit his uncle's title. After leaving school, she had taken a cookery course at Prue Leith's and 'chalet-girled' in Switzerland. She was therefore used to cooking three meals a day for twelve and would have no difficulty in catering for Piggy's massive appetites.

Not a Very Nice Man

5

Piggy Atherstone was a fat, slothful mischief-maker. An advocate of pyramid selling, he had an infuriating habit of trying to flog water purifiers and costume jewellery at dinner parties the instant the Belgian chocolates began to orbit. He also earned an inflated retainer by bringing in non-existent punters to his cousin Gervase's Cork Street art gallery.

Piggy had often been described as 'appetite on trotters'.

He couldn't see a pheasant in his uncle's woods without imagining the poor thing plucked and simmering on a bed of Calvados and sliced Coxes. He also kept his mouth wide open during food fights at parties.

Even worse, Piggy was dreadfully stingy. He never tipped the servants and he stole the Christian Aid envelopes from the porches of hostesses. He was far too mean to buy Araminta an engagement ring – even a cheapie from stock – until they were officially engaged. This would have to be within the next few months because Piggy was determined to be married to her by her twenty-first birthday in September, so that he could get his greedy trotters on all the cash.

Araminta, who was a romantic at heart, had only agreed to marry Piggy because he seemed to be the only man in the world who hadn't slept with her mother – not, had she known it, for want of trying.

Worst of all, Piggy was a tedious chatterbox. Donkeys clung onto their hind legs every time he opened his mouth. The only time he ever got to first base with a girl was by boring the pants off her.

Cast Not Earls Before Swine

6

ere is Piggy boring, and playing bridge with, Rufus Atherstone, Rufus's sister-in-law Amelia, and Hetty, Amelia's friend from London, who played regularly with Omar Sharif. They had had a delicious lunch earlier but, once again, the moment it was over, the little pipsqueak started his pitch and managed to sell a frightful gold necklace to Hetty. Knowing that the way to a woman's hearts, clubs, spades and diamonds was by looking, Amelia held her cards closer to her chest to stop Piggy cheating.

The two women were now quietly confident of a grand slam. Rufus longed to sleep. Piggy was getting seriously on his nerves and his gouted foot was throbbing. He detested the way Piggy clicked his fingers at the maids to bring him a glass of whisky, and then had the cheek to complain that it would taste much better if Rufus would only install a water purifier.

The Earl was filled with despair to think that once Piggy and Araminta were married, this frightful youth would be hanging around Flatgrove pontificating all the time. Perhaps he could flog the smaller Lawrence and buy them a place in Tasmania.

A-Hunting We Will Go

7

'Do you bonk with the Addlebury?'
'No, I bonk with the Berkeley.'

Hunting is the perfect upper-class sport — involving glamorous fancy dress, danger, lots of dogs, a distinct element of cruelty and extensive opportunity for under-covert activity.

Rufus Atherstone owned the Addlebury Hunt, which went very fast, as Lincolnshire was very flat. Although he had to be tied onto his horse, Rufus never missed a day out. Towards the end of March, the Addlebury met at Flatgrove.

25

As the riders devoured home-made sausage rolls and fruit cake and knocked back indifferent port (because Drinkwater had finished the Cockburns), everyone was gossiping about Major Hiccup, who had finally left home.

'I really love Elspeth Hole-Hogg,' he had announced to his wife Blodwyn the previous night.

'I really love Elspeth too,' agreed Blodwyn warmly, because Elspeth was her best friend.

'No, I mean, I really, really love Elspeth,' insisted Hiccup, who had promptly rung for one of the maids to pack his suitcase and driven off.

Today, as though nothing had occurred, Hiccup, Blodwyn and Elspeth were all out hunting. Hiccup, who was suffering from cock-burn after a vigorous night's sport, had, however, just been given a wigging.

'You can't be Joint Master and set *such* a bad example,' roared Rufus.

'You and Flappy have been setting a bad example for years,' protested Hiccup.

'I am an Earl and I own the Hunt,' snapped Rufus.

Today everyone was also gossiping about the poor Queen having to pay tax. Rufus was delighted. He felt there shouldn't be one law for the very, very rich and another for the very, very, very rich.

Rufus was hopping mad with Araminta that day. Not only did he suspect that she'd been helping the hunt saboteurs to unstop earths, but she was supposed to be walking two hunt puppies and Flappy had dropped in the previous evening and found them all sprawled on the sofa in front of a roaring fire, eating chocolate biscuits and watching *Huckleberry Hound* on television. No wonder the Addlebury never caught any foxes if hounds kept escaping from the pack and rushing home for tea at Araminta's.

And, oh bugger, here were the hunt saboteurs in person, throwing firecrackers, blowing hunting horns and even attempting to pull people off their horses.

The saboteurs who tried to unmount Rufus had no luck because he was tied onto his chestnut mare. On the other hand, the beefy, bearded youth who toppled Grace Atherstone only emerged with buckling legs from the undergrowth two days later.

Piggy Atherstone had also turned up at the meet to rub his plump thighs against all the prettiest women and guzzle any leftover port, like the parson at Holy Communion. He soon scuttled home, however, because he was having his portrait painted in his red coat with his horse. This was so that, as the future heir, he might hang in the Long Gallery at Flatgrove and leer at the Titian Madonna.

With One Bounder . . .

8

A large number of pretty women had turned out with the Addlebury that morning because of a false rumour that Bounder Cartwright might be hunting.

Bounder's name hung on everyone's lips like croissant crumbs, because no one was richer, smarter or more glamorous. If Piggy Atherstone was 'appetite on trotters', Bounder Cartwright was 'sex on Lamborghini wheels'. In five seconds he could go from nought to sixty miles per hour.

He was rumoured to have parents in San Francisco but, as with great beeches that cling to yellow Cotswold banks and conceal their roots behind ferns and strands of ivy, his origins were rather obscure. No one minded, however, because Bounder had arrived in London in the early eighties, trailing polo ponies and oodles of dosh and promptly landed a plum-in-the-mouth job with a merchant banker in the City.

The job didn't last. Returning one day from a three-hour lunch, he was so plastered that his two companions put him into the window cleaners' cradle on the pavement outside the bank to sleep it off. Alas, later in the day, the cradle was tugged up to the sixth floor, where a board meeting was in progress. Poor Bounder was roused by the red roaring face of the chairman yelling out of the window: 'This is as high as you're going to get in this firm, Cartwright.'

So Bounder decided employment wasn't for him and put all his money into the stock exchange and Lloyds. Working from home, he grew even richer. Lying in his bath till lunch-time, like Joan Collins and Grace Atherstone, Bounder did deals; rang Switzerland, Liechtenstein and the Cayman Islands on his mobile; and was up to every fiddle.

'Thank havens for little tax,' sang Bounder in his bath.

He also threatened to turn the *Financial Times* even pinker by gossiping intimately with his cohorts of women friends, none of whom he'd had any trouble attracting. Languid, lean, watchful, utterly still, Bounder was *lurcherous* rather than lecherous. He moved in so swiftly that a mesmerised admirer was post-coital before she could ring nine, nine, nine, or, if she were German, like the Royal Family, say, 'Nein, nein, nein.'

Bounder was also multi-phasic.

'I don't mind him watching television while he makes love to me,' complained one beauty, 'but I wish he wouldn't change channels, close deals and shout, "I'm Cayman" at the moment of orgasm.'

But it never seemed to deter any of them.

Bounder was looked after by a man called Tonio, who cleaned his flat, walked his dogs, ran his bath, brushed his numerous suits, few of which had been paid for, and polished his numerous pairs of shoes, which had been specially made to fit his long, narrow, gentlemanly feet.

Bounder had a delinquent lurcher called Hooligan Long-tail. Even while pretending to be asleep on the bathmat, Hooligan would be planning his next misdemeanour.

Like most yuppies, Bounder had cleaned up in the eighties. Then, suddenly, at the end of 1992, he found himself gutted by disasters at Lloyds and the collapse of the property and stock markets.

On March 30th 1993 the bailiffs repossessed his beloved Lear jet and all his houses except for the Knightsbridge flat. Nor, having cuckolded most of them, could he expect his men friends to bail him out. Indeed, not many of them could have afforded to. Lloyds had decimated the upper classes more effectively than any revolution. You could hear the tumbrils rumbling down Kensington Gate. Bounder toyed with the idea of marketing a tumbril drier.

It was a bleak day for Bounder. Fed up with not being paid for six months, Tonio had finally walked out. Consequently the flat was a tip.

'None shall sweep,' Bounder sang along with Pavarotti in his bath.

Pulling a Fast One

9

Such setbacks didn't alter the habits of a lifetime. Bounder still went to Newmarket.

Thank goodness Broker's Blues was a dead cert in the 2.30. Having had a hot tip, Bounder put fifty thousand pounds, which he hadn't got, on the colt. That should get him out of the wood.

Over in the Paddock, Broker's Blues's four owners and his jockey stood together in an isolated island. Making reassuring

noises like the bride's father before a trip up the aisle, the trainer had moved off to check his other horse in the race. The owners closed in. Bounder's bet had been overheard. This was the gang that laid the plot that pulled the colt which was backed by Bounder Cartwright. The three men, braying telegraph poles in floppy hats, had all been cuckolded by Bounder; the woman had been dropped by him untimely.

'Don't worry, old chap,' they whispered to the jockey. 'We don't mind if Broker's Blues isn't even placed.'

The big race was in several weeks' time and they wanted to fix the odds — and Bounder. And to Bounder's dismay and ruination, Celibate Celia lolloped home five lengths clear, with Broker's Blues nowhere.

'Dear Lord, may I lose less frequently but more gracefully,' prayed Bounder.

The only answer was to find a very rich wife; in emulation of his friend Paddy Ponsonby-Porter, who was getting married on Saturday to a girl called Polly-Esther, whose father was making pots of money as a receiver. Meanwhile, Bounder had found a way temporarily to appease his bank manager, a Mr Grasping of the Gnat-Wasp (so called because they were always stinging their customers for massive interest). As Mr Grasping wanted Saturday afternoon off to play golf, Bounder agreed to take his wife Gertie to the wedding. Gertie Grasping was a fearful snob, who was dying to meet not only the Ponsonby-Porters but also the notorious Princess Midas. As a cousin of the bride, the Princess was expected to be among the guests.

Bounder at the Wedding

10

In the red with blood so blue,
Paddy marries money new.

Paddy Ponsonby-Porter's father had, like Bounder, been cleaned out by Lloyds and had just had to sell the farm, the house in Tuscany and the Canalettos. Paddy's female relations were deeply gloomy about the whole wedding. They all wore black and it didn't even occur to them to giggle during the hymn, 'Praise My Soul', at the reference to 'our fathers in distress'.

As they came out of the church, one of Polly-Esther's

sweet little bridesmaids announced that there was 'an enormous marquis' on the lawn.

'Can't be one of the bride's relations,' sniffed old Lady Ponsonby-Porter, who was making no attempt to disguise her feelings. 'I know Polly-Esther's pretty, but a pretty face doesn't disguise the fact that she comes from Surrey, and did you see her mother? Even the bag and shoes were shocking pink. And her father tried to make Paddy wear a bright red carnation with half Epsom Downs behind it. He's already taken off his morning coat. At any minute he'll say "Cheers" and start throwing confetti. He's a receiver, I'm told. They're evidently the only people making money at the moment, except divorce lawyers. Paddy'll certainly need one of those the instant Lloyds recovers.'

But no one listened to her except her little dog. All the men were still imagining Polly-Esther's all-over Nassau suntan beneath her low-cut wedding dress, and wishing they were forty-five years younger. Polly-Esther was worth at least three million.

Bounder would have loved to have spent the wedding chatting up Sukie Ponsonby-Porter, who was at RADA with Polly-Esther. But his sights had to be set on the Princess Midas.

The Midas Touch

11

The English upper-class male has always been fascinated by rich American women: Isabel Archer, Jennie Churchill, Caroline Wedgewood-Benn, Jerry Hall, Ivana Trump. Women like this can bring new blood, high spirits and oodles of cash into the family.

Light years ahead financially of anyone else at the wedding, the Princess Midas was totally recession-proof. A Miss Schlock from Pittsburgh, who had married a Mediterranean princeling, she had kept the Prince's billions and his title when he died.

The Princess Midas was a fine example of the *nouveau* adage that you can never be too thin or too rich. Ignoring the bride, the entire wedding turned towards her like flowers towards the sun, affording her the same apprehensive, sycophantic grins of adoration they would normally only give to royalty. All the Princess ever saw in life was teeth, never behinds, because people always backed out of her presence. They also waited for her to speak first, then hung on her most trivial utterance.

'If she shakes my hand, I may turn to gold.'

Princess Midas insisted that everyone call her 'Mammon'.

Gertie Grasping, in her red-and-black striped dress, was in raptures. If only she could get the Princess as a customer, then Hubby could write off the bank's Third World debt.

Bounder wished he could make it with the Princess. It would solve all his problems. But her disdainful glance made him feel as though he'd left his balls in another suit. And he suspected that if the Princess allowed him to play polo all summer, hunt four days a week, keep racehorses and ride in point-to-points, she'd also expect him to spend his evenings with her. Close up, she was older – and had more stitches in her face – than the Bayeux Tapestry. Bounder bottled out.

An Advance Guard of Aunts

12

hen he caught sight of a quartet of Atherstone aunts. Rufus Atherstone had eighteen sisters. Known as the Juggernaunts, four of them had been invited and had rumbled down from Lincolnshire for the wedding because their youngest sister had married a Ponsonby-Porter.

They'd never been to Surrey before. They were keeping an open mind. If it wasn't too bad, next year they might even venture as far as Essex. At least there was plenty of delicious food and buckets of champagne at the wedding because *nouveaux* always over-cater.

None of the Juggernauts had any intention of tightening their belts in a time of recession. Aspasia billowed like a Weybridge balcony. She was feeling very chipper because her grandson had just got a scholarship to Eton, so she wouldn't have to fork out for the school fees — unlike her sisters, who were green with envy. Monica was reading out a letter from her sister Leonora, deploring the fact that Grace Atherstone's new lover was an undertaker.

'With a willy this big,' demonstrated Rowena.

'One can't know an undertaker socially,' chuntered Monica.

'What with suicides, strokes, heart attacks and Aids,' said Aspasia, 'they're the only people making any money these days.'

'Except receivers and divorce lawyers,' intoned Granny Ponsonby-Porter.

Ann Scott-James once interviewed Nancy Mitford.

'Am I U?' she asked bravely.

'Well, you have U legs,' said Miss Mitford, kindly.

In the same way, the Juggernauts have never considered themselves fat because they have thin ankles.

Fortunately, the 'enormous marquis' was big enough to accommodate all the guests, including the four aunts, who were determined to enjoy themselves. They even stayed on for the dance after the bride and bridegroom had left for South Africa – in the Lear jet which the bride's father's bailiffs had repossessed from Bounder back in March.

'If you're so broke,' murmured Sukie Ponsonby-Porter to a saddened Bounder, 'why don't you try to detach Araminta from Piggy Atherstone. They're not officially engaged. She'd solve your problems.'

If Araminta was anything like her aunts, reflected Bounder, she didn't sound the sort of girl who'd cramp a chap's style. And if her father owned half of Lincolnshire, think of the hunting and shooting. Bounder also remembered his friend Luis Basualdo's advice.

'Don't go for beautiful young girls, they're fickle; marry homely, chubby girls. They'll always look after you, and you can bed the pretty ones in the afternoon.'

By the end of the evening, Bounder had ingratiated himself by dancing with each of the Juggernaunts, Monica, Leonora, Rowena and Aspasia. This was rather like steering four overloaded trolleys round Sainsbury's in swift succession. He emerged from this ordeal with an invitation to Aspasia's house, Jollity Court, in a fortnight's time.

Love Among the Lurchers

13

Jollity Court could be very daunting. Aspasia and her husband Bing were very cosy. But they had a lot of very glamorous, noisy and self-assured friends.

Although flesh was considered flash, on Saturday night many of the women wore dresses cut lower than Polly-Esther's wedding dress, in the hope of ensnaring Bounder. In fact, so many guests of both sexes blow-dried their hair in anticipation, that they blew the fuses of the entire house instead.

Poor relation Priscilla, from Northumberland, who'd never stayed at Jollity Court before, was so terrified at the prospect of charades later, she could hardly eat a mouthful of dinner. There is an element of sadism about country house charades. On such occasions, Flashman is alive and well and, if not exactly roasting poor little eighteen-year-olds from Northumberland over the fire, is likely to order them to get up and act out 'A second term at Lindy St Clair's' in front of a crowd of neighing strangers. If you merely suggest the name of a book, a song or a film, you're regarded as being a boring drip.

Poor Priscilla, having drunk six times too much at dinner to calm her nerves, was dying to spend a penny when the time came to act, of all nightmarishly embarrassing things: 'Just popping down to the blow-job centre.'

Bounder was given 'A bulimic in a china shop' to portray. After three snorts of coke, he brought the house down by pretending to throw up in every cache-pot.

Cocks and clocks went forward that night. Poor Priscilla was so petrified that Bounder would nip into her bedroom on his whistle-stop tour along the passages, that she spent the night in an armchair pushed against the door. Aunt Aspasia always put her male guests in a bedroom next to that of their bird of the moment so if they slept together the maids wouldn't suspect anything and ring the *News of the World*.

During the evening, Araminta's lurcher Lightning, despite being frightened upstairs by the cracker bangs, fell madly in love with Bounder's lurcher, Hooligan Longtail, who had dined on most of the stable cats.

Apologising for Hooligan's behaviour, Bounder explained that his dog was very bored because the coursing season was over. But Aunt Aspasia couldn't have cared less. 'There isn't a songbird left in Lincolnshire because of those wretched cats,' she said.

Bounder was lucky that Araminta didn't overhear this conversation. She both loved cats and thought coursing was horribly cruel. But she stayed in her bedroom all evening in floods of tears because Ashdown and Mellor, the two hound puppies which she had looked after since October, had had to go back to the hunt kennels earlier in the day. April was the cruellest month.

Hardly Anyone for Tennis

14

Everyone had had such a gaudy libidinous night, few made the tennis court the next day. Priscilla wore dark glasses to hide her reddened eyes and flannel trousers to cover her awful legs. Zuleika, in the big hat, wore dark glasses to hide the ravages of a night with Bounder. All the dogs were eyeing the last stable cat, who had taken refuge from Hooligan Longtail on Zuleika's knee.

That faddy foodie, Piggy Atherstone, was busily reading

the restaurant reviews in the Sunday papers, salivating over which restaurant he'd live in once he'd got his trotters on Araminta's trust fund. Convinced that Zuleika, who smelled more exotic than the colour magazines, was making eyes at him from behind those dark glasses, he envied the cat, lying in her lap. About to get stuck into the Pimm's he was glad to see reinforcements coming out from the house.

Araminta, who had cheered up since last night, was dying to get onto the court.

'Come on, Priscilla,' she urged, 'we'll be half a stone lighter after a couple of sets. Let's work off some of the flab, then we'll be able to have seconds of the chef's *tarte aux pommes*. I promise Mikey isn't frightening, he never minds losing.'

This was a complete lie. Mikey played every night during the week at Queen's and, like most old Etonians, was more competitive than John McEnroe. He would exterminate Priscilla if she missed a ball or served a double fault. And if they looked like losing, he would very likely fake a sprained ankle.

'Go on, Priscilla,' urged Piggy, who wanted the Pimm's and Zuleika to himself. 'You can ballboy,' he added to the little yuppy in the eyeshade, who was dying to play too.

Araminta's partner Charlie managed to swing his aces past her bulk and they beat Priscilla and a foaming Mikey six–love, six–love.

'Lendl's no good on grass either,' Araminta told Priscilla kindly.

As they came off the court, Bounder was just getting up. Looking out of the window as far as his bloodshot eyes could see, everything belonged to Rufus Atherstone: even Jollity Court was part of the estate, temporarily leased to Aspasia and Bing. As lunch wasn't *placé*, Bounder managed to sit next to Araminta and they talked lurchers.

Hooligan Longtail, having polished off his hostess's Buff Orpingtons and one of Piggy's Gucci loafers, was sleeping it off on Lightning's beanbag. Lightning gazed at him adoringly. Perhaps they could meet and mate when Lightning came into season. Araminta gazed adoringly at Bounder.

'I don't know why you like lurchers,' scoffed Piggy, who was devouring a fourth helping of *tarte aux pommes*. 'They're just mongrels, not even recognised breed dogs.'

'Rubbish,' said Bounder. 'I can always recognise Hooligan Longtail in a crowd. He's the one with a mouthful of feathers.'

Araminta laughed and laughed.

Bounder left thirty pounds, which he could ill afford, in his bedroom as a tip for the servants. In revenge for the put-down, Piggy Atherstone nipped in and stole it. One didn't want the servants getting ideas and it would enable him to take Zuleika out for a modest night on the tiles.

A Brush with Memories

15

Araminta couldn't stop thinking about Bounder. Before he left for London, she would have liked to have taken him to meet Pansy, her favourite aunt. It was Pansy who had given her father the Madonna book and who lived in a pretty house nearby. Pansy, however, had gone to her art class.

Widowed after a *mariage blanc*, Pansy had found life rather dull. Golf was too energetic, bridge beyond her, so she had taken up her paintbrush. Now a world of excitement unfolded, still life one day, life drawing the next.

Quintin, the male model, was a magnificent specimen — like one of the statues at Flatgrove. Pansy would have liked to have placed him by the ha-ha. How did he manage to stay so still, she asked, offering him a cup of coffee from her Thermos. Quintin, a resting (not to say, arresting) actor, admitted that he preferred to model lying down: such good practice for playing a corpse in Shakespearean tragedy.

Aunt Pansy couldn't stop squinting at Quintin. She didn't remember having seen anything quite like that before. What did it remind her of? Something that had made a great impression a long time ago. Or was it? She must get Mr Mower to cut back the wisteria round the dining-room window tomorrow.

The art master, with whom the entire class were in love, told Pansy she *must* concern herself with perspective rather than dimension.

An Unwelcome Guest

16

The recession was biting so hard that Gervase Ponsonby-Porter came down from London to see his Aunt Pansy for the first time in ten years. Everyone except Araminta was tearing their hair out because Aunt Pansy planned to leave her vast fortune to the National Canine Defence League on condition that they found a home for Muffin, her little dog, if she died before him.

Gervase, however, was determined to squeeze half a

million out of Pansy to shore up his Cork Street gallery. The Hockneys he'd paid fifty thousand for last week had turned out to be fakes. Two backers had gone belly up last week and Piggy Atherstone, whom he employed to bring in rich punters, had produced nothing but vast restaurant bills.

Grand, slothful, self-important, silly, Gervase was so vain he gave his mirror stubble-trouble. Over the years, some of the most beautiful women in London had hung like chain bags on his arm at parties, at the theatre and especially at the ballet. All so beautiful, he informed Aunt Pansy, with a force-ten sigh, that he could never choose between them.

In fact, he was merely their walker, and had a string of discreet boyfriends. His latest, Ninian, was having an exhibition entitled 'Pop Goes the Easel' at the gallery next month. Ninian, whose real name was Nige, was actually a house painter whose talents lay in the bedroom — another reason Gervase needed an injection of cash from Aunt Pansy.

Pansy, who had always believed Gervase was 'bi-spec-tacled', thought he had come down because he wanted to mount an exhibition of her water-colours, but Gervase, whose philosophy was 'Never Apologise, Never Admire,' whisked round her studio emitting more force-ten sighs and only pausing for a second to clock her painting of Quintin. When pressed for an opinion, he murmured that while art could be abstract and should certainly be cathartic, he felt Aunt Pansy's paintings verged on the syrup-of-figurative.

Once stuck into the Dom Perignon, however, he banged on and on and on. 'In our house in Provence, Ninian and I have to shut the windows at two in the morning to stop the nightingales keeping us awake. But, as Harold Acton wrote about the nightingale . . .'

'Acton, Acton,' interrupted Aunty Pansy peevishly, 'I've never been to Acton, I don't think I'd like it.'

'The way to improve as a painter,' Gervase cut across her again, as he handed her an invitation to Ninian's private view, 'is to study others' work.'

'But what does it mean?' asked Aunt Pansy, gazing in bewilderment at a large khaki blob on the card.

'Never ask what a painting means,' chided Gervase. 'Say instead: "Does it convey an emotional truth?" Ninian's paintings,' his voice flowed on like the Tiber, 'are far finer in the flesh, as is Ninian. Luminous, numinous, superficially vague, they are passionate, triumphant reaffirmations remote from real life's concerns and immediately relevant just because of that.'

What *was* he talking about? Poor Muffin grew cross-eyed with boredom too.

'Ninian's very stressed out,' explained Gervase as Aunt Pansy examined Ninian's sulky photograph on the back of the invitation card. 'He simply refused to *dire fromage*. Small wonder, when the poor lad is starving in a garret.'

Gervase then made his pitch for half a million.

With that girth, reflected Aunt Pansy, Gervase himself was certainly not starving in the Garrick. It was cruelty to Muffin to have to listen to this pompous ass any longer. Pansy was even more determined than ever to leave everything to the National Canine Defence League. If she didn't kick Gervase out soon, she'd have to invite him to supper and miss *Coronation Street*.

The Wooing of Araminta

17

Gervase returned to London absolutely livid with Aunt Pansy and ordered even cheaper wine than usual for Ninian's opening. Everyone turned up to get their photographs in *Hello!* and the *Tatler* and to see their friends. Only wallflowers look at paintings at gallery parties. No one bought anything. The only red spot was on Piggy's forehead because he'd eaten a whole box of Belgian chocolates the previous night.

Araminta really oughtn't to wear a short skirt with calves like that, reflected Bounder, who for once had arrived at a party on time. His Knightsbridge flat had finally been repossessed. The mortgage company had even taken Hooligan's beanbag. Bounder's debts were so awful, he must make a serious pitch for Araminta.

'How's Aunt Pansy getting to the party?' asked Araminta.

'By tube,' snapped Gervase.

'Surely you don't want a poor old lady like Pansy crossing Piccadilly by herself in the rush hour?' said Araminta, indignantly.

'Only if a 22 bus runs her over,' snarled Gervase.

Even Bounder was shocked. As the Lamborghini had been repossessed and he couldn't drink any more of Gervase's Corked Street red, he whisked off to collect Pansy in a hired Porsche.

Up from Lincolnshire, turning beetroot in the central heating, was Major Hiccup, back – natch – with his wife, who was managing to look daggers at the beauty Hiccup was ogling, and glare disapprovingly at the black-trousered bottom of Gervase's PA Primrose, to whom Piggy Atherstone was trying to sell a water purifier. Pity he couldn't purify the wine.

Catalogue in hand, a woman from Christie's, there to keep an eye on the competition, was amazed that Gervase could exhibit such junk. Gertie Grasping's sister, in the white shoes, was searching for a cerise-and-royal-blue blob to match the cerise-and-royal-blue décor in her lounge.

All the men with saluki faces, in dark suits they hadn't paid for, were screwing up their eyes, pretending to look at the paintings closely and whispering out of the corners of their mouths.

'Have you heard? Gervy's just dumped Ninian. He came home last night, found a frite-fly good-looking burglar pocketing the silver and asked him to move in. Gervy said the boy's knowledge of books, paintings and antiques is positively encyclopaedic.'

Gervase, meanwhile, was banging on to anyone who'd listen about the absolute *thing* Picasso had for Princess Margaret and about Barbara Hepworth, who was 'so instinctively artistic', even when she threw down a tea towel it fell in the right folds.

'Good Mauling,' sourly he greeted the art critic from the *Guardian*, who'd rubbished his previous exhibition.

The party broke up early because poor dumped and reviled Ninian had locked himself in the lavatory threatening suicide, so everyone had to beetle off down the road to the Ritz in order to have a pee.

As they were all leaving, Aunt Pansy arrived, singing Bounder's praises: 'Such a charming young man: met me in a porch at Green Park, playing music so loudly I could really hear it.'

In order that she could play Gilbert and Sullivan *sforzando* without frightening Muffin, Bounder had suggested she invest in a CD Walkman. Piggy and Gervase, who still cherished considerable expectations of Aunt Pansy, nearly fainted when she announced delightedly that Bounder was going to find her a 'Seedy Walker'.

As Piggy was still doing a number on Primrose, Bounder whisked Araminta out to the Porsche, in the back of which lay Hooligan Longtail collapsed in exquisite folds, pretending to be a Barbara Hepworth tea towel. Hooligan certainly conveyed an emotional truth. So did the salmon fishcakes at Annabel's where Bounder and Araminta had dinner. Later they admired Mark Birley's dog paintings.

'The dreadful thing about being an aristocrat,' sighed Araminta, looking up at a picture on the wall of a springer spaniel carrying a grouse, 'is that one's relations are all serial killers. My father makes Hannibal Lecter or the Yorkshire Ripper look like Mother Theresa. All his life he has murdered grouse, pheasant, snipe, partridge, ptarmigan, salmon, trout, foxes, hares and deer.'

'Each man kills the thing he loves,' said Bounder, smoothly. 'The coward does it with a kiss.'

Araminta wished Bounder would kiss *her*. Dreamily she confided that she had always longed to be proposed to at Annabel's while the band played 'Our Love is Here to Stay', which was the cracked 78 her father often played on his wind-up gramophone because it reminded him of Grace.

Bounder took Araminta off to dance.

'Who was Annabel?' asked the Princess Midas, who was dining in a dark corner with Grace Atherstone's undertaker.

'Wasn't he the bloke what came over the Alps on an elephant?' said the undertaker, who was staring in utter amazement at Araminta's bulk.

Then the band played 'Our Love is Here to Stay', and Bounder asked Araminta to marry him.

'Have you ever been to bed with my mother?' gasped Araminta.

'Never, never,' Bounder shook his sleek, dark head.

'Do you promise Hooligan will give up coursing? I don't want him leading Lightning astray.'

For half Lincolnshire, twenty million and the Titian Madonna, Bounder agreed he could make this sacrifice.

'Then, yes, I will,' cried Araminta joyfully.

As Araminta had to break it off with Piggy and Bounder had to ask her father's permission, they agreed not to tell anyone yet except Bounder's bank manager and Nigel Dempster.

As Bounder's flat had been repossessed, the possession of Lightning Atherstone by Hooligan Longtail took place later at the Turf Club.

eatime Tristesse

18

She that kisses the toy boy as he flies
Lives in Eternity's sunrise.

Elvira, Charlotte and Corinna were desperately depressed by rumours of Bounder's engagement. Sad women without husbands, or with husbands philandering in London; Bounder had been their lifeline. They had their gardens and their dogs, but sometimes that wasn't enough. They wanted a little love too.

The loneliness of Elvira, Charlotte and Corinna was tangible. Hemmed in by hedges like great blocks of frozen spinach, they were mocked by balls and phallic symbols. The yew peacock of their pride was grounded. It was only Monday and the week stretched ahead. It was only four-thirty but they'd be stuck into the Muscadet long before six.

Elvira's husband had just walked out on her.

'The badgers got at the dustbins,' she told her companions. 'And there was Grace Atherstone's passionate letter to Johnnie hardly torn up and scattered all over the drive for the maids and the gardeners to see. When I confronted him, he just left home.'

Charlotte was unhappily married to a compulsive womaniser.

'Eddie said he couldn't live with himself if he left me, so now we're a ghastly *ménage à trois*: Eddie, himself and me. The bank manager advised us to sell the house in Lincolnshire and the flat in Pelham Crescent and buy a maisonette in Loughton so Eddie could commute to the City every day. "Don't you want to save your marriage?" he said, seeing me whiten close to death. "Not that much," I said dolefully.'

Corinna, widowed and on her own, had been to a dance the previous night.

'I was left alone at the table with this businessman. When

I screwed up courage and asked him to dance, he said, "I only dance with twenty-year-olds, but I don't mind talking to you." It's at times like that I miss Rory most.'

'It's all right for you, Corinna,' snapped Elvira, 'Rory only died. You never had to suffer the humiliation of him walking out.'

Women without men in the husband-haunted yew corridors. We're all in the same boat, they are thinking. It'll sink soon, there are so many of us. But one can't commit suicide if one has dogs. Brought up by Nanny; shunted off to boarding school; abandoned by Johnnie, Eddie and Rory. In the end, it's only the dogs that stay faithful.

The Fourth of June

19

Cousin Rosalind was spitting. It was Dommie's first term at Eton and Jeremy, who'd put her on a stupid cash diet, had assured her no one bothered very much at the Fourth of June.

'Look, typical,' she fumed. 'The Foxe-Whapshotts have not only brought their butler so they don't ruin their lovely new clothes, but they've got the family silver out and the damask tablecloth and the most wonderful wines. And you said it would be all right to put coffee in a Thermos and bread and cheese would do. And now they're handing round gulls' eggs. I'll show them next year.'

It was all right for Jeremy. He didn't resent other parents' more lavish picnics. He was happy admiring other people's dogs and the constant procession of ravishingly pretty little sisters.

Dommie, on the other hand, was so mortified by his parents' frugality that he hadn't been seen all day.

Everyone was talking about Araminta and Bounder. Bounder's myriad ex-girlfriends were distraught. The flag was at half-mast at Annabel's. The tear level was rising at San Lorenzo; soon the restaurant would be under salt water.

People at the Fourth of June were still obsessed with the recession and the nightmare of paying the school fees. Grannies were expected to fork out for Eton, but would they also cough up for a university? If you couldn't get into Oxbridge, then Edinburgh, Newcastle and Exeter were the only possible choices.

Granny Hiccup was not amused. She was paying for Tertius Hiccup's school fees and when she had asked him what he was going to do when he left, he laughed and said: 'Be a sex maniac, like daddy.'

Dommie said the silly thing about Eton was that if you were caught in bed with a girl, you got sacked, but if you were caught with a boy you got two hours' gardening.

Eco and Narcissus

20

ousin Caspar had spent so many hours gardening at Eton that he took it up as a career. Normally, he designed gardens in Richmond, Ham, Putney and also St John's Wood – where he had been much praised for a rock garden which looked like an exploded meteorite. But the recession and a beastly letter from Mr Grasping, *insisting* that he instantly reduce his borrowings, drove him down to the country to discuss the possibility of redesigning

Aunt Cecily's garden.

Caspar loathed country gardens. Nothing but boring boxes of box with pastel flowers spilling out of them. And Cecily had gone seriously organic. She'd banned artificial fertilisers, chemical sprays and peat, so one couldn't just bang in a few rhododendrons – and she now swore by FYM, as she called farmyard manure. The only thing on which she was prepared to use slug pellets was Piggy Atherstone.

Having trailed round Aunt Cecily's garden, getting his Guccis caked in mud, Caspar was now being besieged by her ghastly dogs, who had covered his beautiful suit with hairs, and he was sure half of them had rolled in FYM.

And now Cecily was going on and on about herbal remedies in her new herb garden: 'This is Araminta's lurcher, who's suffering from morning sickness. I'm going to try her on camomile tea.'

The dogs were edging nearer Caspar. Lightning's nose was at cake-level. The dachsie had the fruit cake on the floor.

'Rats, the Norwich terrier,' announced Cecily fondly, 'has turned the lawn into a putting green. I wish I could persuade him to reduce his burrowings.'

'I gather Araminta is going to marry a young man called Bounder?' she asked. 'D'you know anything about him?'

The news made Caspar feel even lower. Girls were almost as ghastly as dogs, but he'd always regarded Araminta as a possible bolt-hole if he got too strapped for cash.

Aunt Cecily was also a staunch supporter of the National

Canine Defence League, like Pansy. In her window was their sticker – 'A Dog is For Life.'

'Oh, *please* no,' thought Caspar with a shudder.

'If dogs were large enough,' said Cecily, 'that nice Bruce Fogle told me, they would regard us as meals, not parents.'

When she went out to answer the telephone, Rats mounted Caspar's leg. Caspar gave such a vicious kick that, rising in a perfect parabola, Rats passed Cecily at eye-level as she returned. Caspar didn't get the job after all.

Elvira, Charlotte and Corinna have perked up. Bounder has asked them all to sleep with him as a wedding present.

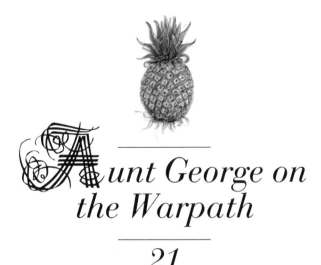

Aunt George on the Warpath

21

When Aunt is calling to Aunt, like Mastodons bellowing across a primeval swamp . . .

P. G. Wodehouse

he FYM had really hit the fan. Aunt George, Piggy Atherstone's widowed mother, had picked up the *Daily Mail* and found a piece in Nigel Dempster's column linking Bounder's name to Araminta's:

'We are in a relationship,' admits junoesque Araminta, only daughter of the Earl of Atherstone (family motto: per ard-on ad astra) and long-time girlfriend of "Piggy"

Atherstone, her father's heir. 'Our lurchers are just good friends,' laughs Araminta.

'Pshaw!' Steam was coming out of Aunt George's ears. ' "In a relationship," indeed. Getting one's name in the tabloids! Disgusting! "Relationship" – *ghastly* word. Sounds like a tanker full of uncles. Pshaw! What is this name, Cartwright? Who was his mother before she was a Cartwright?'

No one seemed to know. Aunt George, who had the permanently outraged expression of a cat being de-fleaed, telephoned her brother Rufus in a rage. But the Earl proved surprisingly stubborn. Bounder was a most amusing fellow, who'd given him a video of the Madonna film, and had promised to take him to a strip club, next time he came up to London.

Piggy also refused to be roused.

'Don't worry, Mumsy. Silly girl's only got a crush on Bounder. Anyway, he's the sort of chap girls always lose, like dark glasses or an umbrella.'

Aunt George was not appeased. And her day went from bad to worse. She had then to go to a show near Spalding to judge the Welsh cobs and was demoted to judging the egg-and-spoon race – and she absolutely *loathed* children. Worse still, wretched Cecily had introduced a gymkhana event to make teenagers more aware of the importance of safe sex. They had to hurtle down the field on their ponies and see who could be the first to put a condom on a yard broom. Disgusting! Pshaw!

The Addlebury Hunt retained Aunt George to act as a security guard to keep saboteurs out at meets. She also chucked-out at hunt balls. Last year a saboteur had chucked a brick at her and the brick was in intensive care for a week.

Knowing dogs were supposed to grow like their owners, Mousie, an incurable optimist, hoped he'd one day turn into a Rottweiler. Trotting beneath Aunt George's undercarriage like a Dalmatian, all he could see were vast quivering thighs encased in navy blue serge. If only they had been Lurex, he could have pretended he was Patrick Moore, gazing up at the night sky.

*P*arty Politics

22

ffie was listening to her favourite Fats Waller and basking in the afterglow of the very successful party she had given to celebrate the engagement (still admittedly unofficial) of her cousin Araminta and Bounder Cartwright.

Effie had been worried that Rosebud Atherstone, who'd put on a huge amount of weight, and all the Juggernauts, wouldn't fit into the flat. So she put away the best pieces of china and glass as one does at a children's party. But the place had been left incredibly tidy, no drink rings or wine stains covered in salt, no broken glasses, no shrieking and slamming of car and taxi doors waking up the whole of the Cadogans when they left. And the *boeuf en croûte* had really worked.

The only blot on the evening had been Piggy Atherstone, who had crashed the party, announcing tragically that he had left two bottles of Krug, bought specially for Effie, on the bus – on which, alas, he was reduced to travelling now Araminta had jilted him and he was going to be so poor. With sobs and sighs, he had then grabbed a glass of less exalted champagne with one hand and a fistful of angels-on-horseback with the other.

Effie was expecting Bounder Cartwright to be another Piggy, but in fact he was drop-dead handsome and enhanced the party, as a pat of *maître d'hôtel* cheers up a rather boring sole. And *so* amusing: he told Effie about the goat called Michael who ate all the cigarette ends overflowing from the ashtrays at the Royal Berkshire Polo Club. He felt Effie could do with a Michael. 'And a Bounder,' he added in an undertone. Then he made a pass at her. Men always did. But Effie said she didn't have *affaires* with engaged men, so why didn't they save it for marriage when Bounder would be much richer.

And it was lovely to think that Bounder, as a member of the family, would add a *frisson* to christenings, weddings and funerals for years to come. All this made Effie's current admirers, particularly Major Hiccup and Cocky Broadstairs, wildly jealous.

Effie had learnt that the secret of happiness was to regard men as a luxury, not a necessity. As the evening progressed, Grace Atherstone had turned up with her latest — a flash Greek flasher called Aristotle Popitoutalot — and he did. And Gervase glided in with his new friend, Boris the Burglar, who had peroxided his hair and moustache blond as a disguise. Boris was seriously good value: he knew everyone and, of course, frequented all the best houses — though not always invited.

Finally, they all went home and Effie was able to give her dogs and cats some quality time and listen to Fats Waller. Then, one after another, the husbands had begun to ring up — from Chelsea, Knightsbridge, Kensington, Wandsworth, Battersea and Clapham — to say they'd dropped a Mogadon in their wife's cocoa and could they come back? But Effie told them all she was exhausted — she was sure Cocky Broadstairs and Major Hiccup didn't believe her — because she wanted to keep the coast clear, just in case, for Bounder. Why else would he have left his Norwich terrier, his Dalmatian and Hooligan Longtail behind, except as an excuse to return? Earlier, the Norwich terrier had done 'trust-and-paid-for' with a bit of *croûte*. Oh, Cousin Araminta, you're going to have to trust-and-pay-for Bounder for the rest of your life.

It *was* a good party, reflected Effie, even though Piggy had passed out in the broom cupboard and Aunt Pansy had sat in a corner all evening, listening to 'Classic FYM', as she insisted on calling it, on her 'Seedy Walker'.

But hark! Effie could hear a purposeful footstep in the hall. Bounder must have returned.

Horrors! It was only Piggy, stripped for action, wearing nothing but a corn plaster.

Mariana's Blues

23

Mariana, Cocky Broadstairs's wife, was seriously depressed. Even her long gentlewoman's feet drooped. Bounder Cartwright was supposed to be dropping in but had obviously stood her up. He always rang beforehand just to check the coast was clear.

Not that Cocky would mind, thought Mariana. He's having such a whirl with Effie. The moment I heard the dull thud

of the hot water on the bubble bath yesterday morning, I knew he was off to see her. And afterwards the bottom of the bath was covered in toenail clippings — talk about a bed of nails.

And all my friends have been ringing up telling me how marvellous Effie's party for Araminta was, and how Bounder's fallen madly in love with Effie, which means: Hooray, she'll chuck Cocky, and aren't I thrilled? Actually, I'm even lower. Cocky rang up this afternoon to say something had just come up — probably him — so he's not coming home this evening. I could hear Fats Waller and giggling in the background, so I said I'd burn the house down and hung up. I don't want a moated grange. I want a motel with Bounder in it. Will he ever ring again or am I lost in the mistresses of time? Oh look, a little postman panting up the drive with a telemessage. Oh bliss, it's from Cocky! That burning-the-house-down ploy must have worked. He must love me after all. . . . Bastard! All it says is: 'Save Mummy's portrait.'

Meet the Plant Aunts

24

Faith and Hope get their kicks from stealing cuttings. They check which gardens are open in the Yellow Book and off they go. In winter all one needs is scissors, and lots of plastic bags in the pocket of one's Husky. In summer, a big bag will do.

Faith is snipping away. Hope is keeping *cave*. The dogs are watching apprehensively. If their mistresses get caught and sent to prison, will they have to go into kennels? Hope had a nightmare the other day that Kipper could talk and sat at the head of the table with his paws folded, telling the entire dinner party whose gardeners she'd been denuding.

Today's gardening spree is at Grace Atherstone's place. Grace has pinched our husbands, thinks Faith, so we're *jolly* well going to nick her cuttings. They'll have a much nicer time with us. The best plants in a garden are always the stolen ones, they get far more attention and treasuring. Certainly more than at Grace's. She's not interested in plants — except Venus fly-trap. So this is a kind of plant rescue. Anyway, we're not digging up the plants, just pruning. We wouldn't do it at the Chelsea Flower Show though: that really *would* be stealing.

We could drop a few French marigold seeds to rot up her white border. When I think of the cuttings we've given away.

Anyway, it's important to reassure oneself one's garden is better than other people's and get new ideas. Let's have a bit of that. I've never seen a phlox that pink before. Gosh, this is fun! I feel sorry for men having to get their kicks from boring old adultery. Now we'd better buzz down to Cecily's before the greenfly eat absolutely everything. Talk about aphidious Albion!

Widows' Weeds

25

*Now is the time for all good women
to come to the aid of the parterre.*

Aunt Bea was hopping mad. Her sister Dymphna had said they had to cut down and promptly sacked Sydney, the under gardener. So now I have to lower myself to these menial tasks, chuntered Bea. I *hate* weeding. I love picking flowers and idly pruning a stray twig with my clippers. But weeding's the end; it'll ruin my hands. I'll just tug the top off. Dymphna'll never notice. She's in a tizz because we're opening tomorrow. Why can't we have a wild garden and grow docks and dandelions everywhere, like the Prince of Wales? Why can't we use weedkiller? Green, green, I loathe you, green.

We used to have ten gardeners here. Now we've only got Mr Hackett. He's over there having a compost mortem with Dymphna. She's livid because he's just dug up a whole bed of alstroemerias. Now he's saying Sydney must have put them in and he doesn't know what's what any more. Hackett's useless. While I was away at the Chelsea Flower Show he strimmed all the cow parsley along the ha-ha (it was no joke), pruned the shrub roses to nothing, and butchered the tree peonies. Why do men love to impose brute force on nature? They're always edging, hacking and cutting down. Hackett says it's getting rid of dead wood. I'll find myself on the bonfire soon.

Hope we get lots of people round tomorrow. At a pound a head, it all helps. Can't think why Dymphna lets in children free. Ought to charge a fiver each to deter the little beasts. Grace Atherstone is *such* a bitch. She deliberately opens Libertine Hall on the same day as us. Last year she kept ringing up on a walkie-talkie, saying she'd had thousands through. We only had five and were left with a hundred and ninety-five doughnuts because we'd offered to do teas. This year Grace'll get even more people because she's prostituted herself giving an interview to *Hello!* She justifies it by saying if the public sees how stunning she and her gardens are, they'll pour in from miles around and spend fortunes in the Gifte Shoppe and rich Americans will queue up to hire the shooting.

Oh, look, there's a busload of slugs on their way to lunch at Cecily's hostas. They don't worry about saying grace: they just get stuck in.

Oh why, oh why didn't *Hello!* ask *us*?

Bounder for the Cup

26

In 1992 the polo bubble burst on the prongs of Andrew Morton's fork. Gone are the days when anyone who was anyone met on the polo field. If they did, they'll be divorced by now.

Once upon a time, a princess had to be so thin-skinned and delicate she was rendered insomniac by a pea hidden under twelve mattresses. Today, if her marriage is to have any chance of surviving, she has to be too thick-skinned to

detect under only one mattress her husband's letters from
his mistress.

In the past, businessmen used to squander fortunes on
polo in the hope of hoisting themselves off the financial
pages and onto the front of *The Times*, brandishing some
huge trophy with Prince Charles. Mecca was high tea at
Highgrove. Now the cost of manning a polo team is so pro-
hibitive that a cheaper and less dangerous way of amassing
a lot of silver cups in the drawing-room is to buy a prize bull.

All is not lost, however. Shorn of its yuppies, gangsters
and *nouveaux* floodlighting the pitch with their jewellery
(much of it flogged to them by Piggy Atherstone), and no
longer chronicled by women novelists, polo may well go back
to being the lovely minority sport it once was.

There was a good crowd at Smith's Lawn. Even if the Prince
of Wales had pulled out of high-goal polo, Bounder had
bought six new ponies on the strength of his impending
marriage to Araminta, and his team had reached the final
of the Alfred Dunhill Queen's Cup.

All the spectators were now pouring onto the field to tread
in divots; to show off their long aristocratic feet; to see who
was about; to make assignations; to give their dogs a chance
to fall in love and — because polo always takes place on the
other side of the field — to catch a glimpse of Bounder or the
umpires, who were sometimes handsome Argentinians in
disguise.

In his youth, Rufus Atherstone had played with Prince Philip and sworn at the umpires and the opposition worse than anyone. Now he complained that polo was going to the dogs because players still swore at the umpires and, even more heinously, twiddled their sticks in the air to indicate a foul, which they had probably manufactured in the first place.

People had never been able to understand why Rufus Atherstone didn't mind Horacio, his Argentinia pro, jumping on all of his wives but, as Rufus pointed out, he could always find another wife, but he'd never find a player as dazzling as Horacio.

Bounder was a dazzling player too and his side won by a whisker. Araminta had never been so excited in her life, nor so proud as when the Queen presented the cup to her betrothed. But she couldn't stay for the celebrations afterwards, because back in Lincolnshire, Lightning had suddenly gone into labour and Araminta had to rush home. Oh, the trauma! Lurchers have such narrow hips and a non-existent threshold of pain.

Araminta would have loved Bounder, or at least Hooligan, to be present at the birth. But Bounder felt this was a time a man ought to spend at his club. And anyway, he told Araminta, he was playing polo down at Cowdray tomorrow.

Bridge Too Far

27

ridge fever was sweeping London. In a recession, it was much cheaper than dining out, and men loved it too: they had even stopped lingering for hours over the port after dinner.

It was also the done thing to drive up to London for lunch, play bridge all afternoon and drive back to the country afterwards.

Once you'd dispatched the children to boarding school, it

was Pleasurama all the way. You could have supper and bridge every night. Everyone played and gossiped at the same time. How Bounder and Effie were inseparable, my dear. How Hooligan Longtail had swallowed another Buff Orpington and stampeded a herd of deer in Windsor Great Park between chukkas yesterday. How Gervase's friend, Boris, now had red hair and a red beard and had burgled Aristotle Popitoutalot, who was so high on coke he didn't realise the television was being nicked while he was watching it.

Aunt Leonora's bridge lunch wasn't going with a swing. She'd organised delicious food. Then wretched Primrose, from Gervase's gallery, who'd just got married, cancelled at the last moment. Said she was dying of gastric flu. In fact, she'd sounded so ill, Leonora had rung up Interflora at once.

As everyone had pushed off to the first day of Wimbledon, Leonora was reduced to ringing up Primrose's successor, a little wimp called Tristan, to make up a four.

Poor terrified Tristan was now wishing he was back being jumped on by Gervase. How could he concentrate with all three women yakking at the tops of their voices, speculating why Bounder hadn't yet bought an engagement ring for Araminta?

Now Leonora was shouting at Marjorie, her partner.

'Right, that's it, Marjorie, I told you to get the trumps out.'

Marjorie: 'Yes, dear.'

Leonora: 'Why did you play the king when you could

have won the trick with the ten?'

Marjorie: 'Yes, dear.'

The dogs were worried that poor Lightning Atherstone was still in labour and they'd never get any tea at this rate.

Love-Forty: Repent in Sorrow

28

orse was to come. Pretty Fiona, with the auburn hair, who hated rows, suggested that they have a quick look at Wimbledon to see who was winning the opening men's singles match. So they turned on the television and there, shock horror, was Primrose, looking the picture of health, despite the rather tarty earrings, and sitting next to — Good God! — Bounder Cartwright!

'She said she was dying,' screeched Leonora. 'Those flowers I sent will do for her funeral when I've finished with her. And there's Cynthia Foxe-Whapshott on her left looking frite-fly disapproving.'

Leonora, Marjorie and Fiona were simply furious, particularly because they longed to be at Wimbledon too. Gazing at bronzed Greek gods in the flesh was even more exciting than pinching cuttings. For what other reason would one possibly go that far south-west of the river?

We ought to be there, thought Leonora, Marjorie and Fiona. Wimbledon's such good training for dinner parties; first you turn to the stranger on your right, then to the one on your left; then right; then left; then right; then left; then you crack up at the most inane behaviour: a player winging a linesman or scratching his head over a botched shot.

And look, there's disgusting Aristotle Popitoutalot, chest hair spilling out of his shirt, leering at the trollop with the big mouth and the cleavage. And look at the vicar's wife on his left, disapproving. And look at those dreadful sunhats with Union Jacks on. Everyone who isn't anyone goes to Wimbledon these days.

Gather Ye Rosebud

29

Bounder Cartwright would never have risked going to Wimbledon if he'd known that Rosebud Atherstone, his future father-in-law's wife, would be there on the same day. When people were not chuntering over Bounder's dreadful behaviour, they were expressing amazement at how fat Rosebud had become, swelling up like a hot-air balloon. Aunts George, Leonora, Dymphna and Aspasia had all sent her copies of *The Belly and Bosom Diet Book,* but Rosebud kept on spreading. And look at her tarty shoes. Leopardskin was last autumn's fashion. But she seemed to glow with happiness.

Spectators kept asking her to remove her hat, but she didn't want Hooligan Longtail, who was pretending to be asleep under Bounder's feet, to mistake it for a Buff Orpington, so she left the Centre Court for some strawberries and was now on her third bowl. Multi-phasic as Bounder, she could smoke, drink and eat at the same time. Her dogs lurked, hoping to lick up the sweet pink cream.

Fortunately for Bounder, Rosebud was too locked into herself really to notice him or Primrose, and there was a power cut at Flatgrove, so Rufus Atherstone, who only liked Miss Sabatini anyway, now Chris Evert had retired, missed seeing him.

The only bad thing was that Bounder had lied to Araminta about playing at Cowdray.

Everyone knows polo ponies have a day off on Monday. But he squared it with her on the telephone by saying he'd been offered tickets at the last moment, and knew she wouldn't have wanted to have been dragged away from Lightning, so he'd asked Primrose.

Everyone else, however, was absolutely furious with Bounder. And Piggy decided to make another pitch for Araminta, so he unearthed an ancient cracker ring from the cuff-link bowl on his dressing-table.

Gertie is Royally Enclosed

30

The recession deepened. You were nobody these days, if you hadn't got a bankruptcy and a couple of receiverships under your belt, and spent a year in Ford Open Prison as one of their many librarians. The Old Etonians drifted down to reception every day to see who else had come in.

The bank had foreclosed on Gervase that morning, raiding his gallery at ten-thirty, just as Boris the Burglar was drifting down from the flat upstairs, pulling heated rollers out of his newly-dyed raspberry pink curls. Boris thought they were after him, but instead they seized all Gervase's pictures.

Bounder was terrified he'd be next. 'Oh, don't receive me,' he sang in his bath.

> *'Buzz off and leave me*
> *How could you treat*
> *A poor chairman so.'*

The only way he could stop the Gnat-Wasp finally pulling the plug on him was to get Grasping Gertie into the Royal Enclosure at Ascot. Fortunately, Bounder had had the foresight to apply to St James's Palace in March. Then, buttonholing three of his girlfriends who'd all been to Ascot for the last eight years, he'd bribed them with offers of extra sex to sponsor the Graspings.

As it was, the Graspings were only allowed into the Royal Enclosure on Friday, and Gertie was told she mustn't wear too huge or outlandish a hat, or show too much flesh, or wear too short a skirt, or she wouldn't be allowed back next year.

Gertie thought the whole thing was very gracious. Even though most of the women in the Royal Enclosure were wearing last year's dress, the colours were far more sharp and vibrant than in the public stands. Skirts were worn on the knee, like the banged tail of a horse. Hats, secured by Velcro and hatpins, stayed on in the fiercest wind without being clutched.

Gertie was very covered up in red with a frilly collar to match her frilly hat and frilly blue-rinsed hair. She was deeply despised by a nearby Vel-Crow.

Mr Grasping wore his top hat on the back of his head and a morning suit with a bright blue waistcoat hanging several inches below the waistband. He kept tucking the tails of his morning coat into his trousers, thinking they were shirt tails.

As Flappy Foxe-Whapshott was banging on and on and on, deploring the riff-raff of parvenus, tour operators and ex-jailbirds, albeit ex-librarians at Ford Prison, that had infiltrated the Royal Box, Boris the Burglar calmly relieved her of a gold bracelet and the famous Foxe-Whapshott pearls.

All the Atherstone family who were at Ascot cut Bounder dead – they were still livid with him for cheating so publicly on Araminta. Nigel Dempster reported that the 'relationship' was off. After Ascot, thought Piggy, fingering his cracker ring, he would offer for Araminta.

Bounder Drops One Brick and Picks Up Another

31

Aunt Clodagh only forgave Bounder because she wanted to know who to back in the big race. Having seen her trounce Broker's Blues at Newmarket so decisively earlier in the year, Bounder had no hesitation in recommending Celibate Celia. Aunt Clodagh had a hundred-pound-each-way bet. Bounder bet considerably more.

Joan, Clodagh's prim friend from London, all in black,

legs firmly crossed, demurely sipping a cup of Earl Grey, couldn't understand how Clodagh had let herself go.

Look at her stumping in from the garden without even washing her hands, and having outlandish bets on that red telephone as if she were Boris Yeltsin. Now she was smoking and stuffing herself with chocolate cake and drinking in the middle of the afternoon, even more like Yeltsin. No wonder her figure had collapsed like the art market. And she was far too familiar with the servants, asking Debbie in to watch the race. No wonder the glasses were smeary.

'Red hat, no knickers,' snorted Clodagh, catching sight of Gertie Grasping returning from the paddock.

Clodagh's language, thought Joan, was enough to make Debbie's hair curl, if nothing else could. Look at the silly old trout brandishing the *Sporting Life* and yelling Celibate Celia home. It served her jolly well right that Broker's Blues, not pulled by his jockey this time, won by six lengths at thirty to one. Celibate Celia was nowhere.

Clodagh's Siamese cat briskly clawed her mistress for wasting money. The white whippet bent his legs. As the race was over, he might get a walk. Now was the time for Joan to announce smugly that she had had a ten-pound bet on Broker's Blues. Debbie, who had also had a one-pound forecast at William Hill, was too embarrassed to show her excitement.

In a rage, Clodagh telephoned Rufus Atherstone. Rufus must kill Araminta's engagement once and for all. Bounder didn't know anything about horses either.

126

The Graspings, having had a one-pound bet each way on Celibate Celia, were equally incensed. Bounder, who had lost twenty thousand pounds, decided prompt action was necessary and turned to Piggy.

'Oh Pig are you willing
To sell for one shilling
Your ring?'
Said Piggy, 'I will.
But I can sell you a much better one
for a bit more.'

But Bounder had gone scorching up the motorway to Lincolnshire to propose formally to Araminta, who thought Piggy's cracker ring was the loveliest thing she'd ever seen, even though it would need to be enlarged a little to fit on her finger.

Together she and Bounder gazed at Lightning's puppies, whose eyes were beginning to open, and decided on a wedding towards the end of September, when the polo season would be over.

Seeing the engagement in the *Telegraph* and *The Times*, Mr Grasping agreed to extend Bounder's credit for another two months, so long as Gertie could have a front pew at the wedding.

Runs and Ruins

32

Out in Athens, Aunts Edith and Margaret learned about the engagement twenty-four hours later, in the foreign edition of the *Daily Telegraph*. Oh dear, they supposed they'd better go and look for a wedding present. Such an effort when it was so hot. They'd spent hours finding something for Mrs J. who was looking after the cottage and Bognor, their beloved basset. They'd settled for a miniature *son et lumière* of the Acropolis which flashed worse than Aristotle Popitoutalot. Scent bought on the boat might have been better. They'd sent a postcard to dear Bognor. Goodness, how they missed him!

Edith and Margaret didn't really like Abroad. The food gave them the runs and all the animals looked so miserable. Just as Majorcan fisherman used to queue up on the quay in the fifties to welcome the loose-legged, easy virtued English typists, now Greek mongrels waited on the beach, rubbing their paws as the English tourists arrived. Every morning Edith and Margaret smuggled their breakfast in a napkin out to the waiting pack. The rest of their time was spent yelling at the owners of emaciated and overloaded horses and donkeys.

Edith had a weak chest. Margaret was quite rich. It would have been sensible for them to live abroad to avoid tax and tuberculosis. But if they were to try and hated it, they feared that neither they nor Bognor would survive the six months of quarantine.

Edith and Margaret were rather disconsolate. They couldn't help noticing that Stavros preferred taking that party of young secretaries from Esher round the Parthenon to them, but they couldn't think why.

'I suppose one day,' mused Edith, 'people will come and look at the ruins of Tunbridge Wells. Thank God, we'll be long gone.'

They moved on from Athens to North Africa, where the

donkeys were even thinner and worse treated. What a surprise when they went out for a drink in a local bar to find their nephew, Gervase, sitting there with a handsome young man with raspberry-pink curls, whom Gervase introduced as *his* nephew!

Three generations: *what* fun! Although Edith and Margaret could have sworn Gervase was an only child – and the nephew had a very strange accent and an earring.

When Edith suggested they all have dinner together, Gervase quickly said he and his nephew were already dining out.

Double Chins and Double Gins

33

Another disappointment for Edith and Margaret came when they rang up Cousin Hubert, the British Ambassador, to tell him about Araminta's and Bounder's engagement. They hoped he'd ask them to supper at the embassy, but Hubert quickly said he'd got some bash on and it was *placé*, so he couldn't invite them as well.

Hubert, like all Atherstone males, was a bit of a

womaniser. The Foreign Office had sent him to North Africa, hoping that a country where women were more covered up might deter him. Their optimism had been misplaced.

An ambassador's wife has to be above suspicion and also above suspecting. Mildred had always turned a blind eye to Hubert's infidelities. Mildred had spent so many hours in reception lines, she could sleep on her feet like an old donkey. At least Hubert didn't beat her with a stick or starve her: he was far too busy gazing down the front of the wife of the Panamanian Ambassador.

Jolly D! The Panamanian Ambassador had stayed at home with gyppy tummy. What a little corker! Although it looked as if there might be some competition from the German Ambassador on her left. It was going to be El Alamein all over again.

Storied Urns and Animated Busts

34

ore Plant Aunts. Guinevere and Hortensia were in the great stompingly Sapphic tradition of women gardeners, with Veronica weeding in the background. Cyril Connolly's description of Vita Sackville-West as Lady Chatterley above the waist and the gamekeeper below, fitted Hortensia perfectly.

Guinevere, Hortensia and Veronica spent a lot of time at house sales looking for statues for the garden. The previous

137

day they had been to Gervase's house sale. No one felt very sorry for him having to sell up, because the old meanie didn't even give the family a discount. Not that there was much left after Boris the Burglar had pillaged his fill.

We never knew Gervase's balls were reconstituted stone. Boris, who'd been rubbing yoghurt into them to age them up, pretended they were genuine – but you couldn't fool us.

It was a dreadful mistake letting our sister Grizel drive us to the sale. She's such a drip. She kept sobbing about Gervase's lions being sold off after they had guarded the terrace for three hundred years. She said she saw a tear trickling down one of the lion's grey stone cheeks. Grizel was wiping her own eyes so frantically, the auctioneer thought she was bidding and sold her a twelve-foot replica of Michelangelo's David *sans* fig-leaf. There's no way we're having *that* in the garden. She'd better pass it on to Araminta as a wedding present.

Then we went on to Major Hiccup's place. He went belly up last week: first time *he's* taken the missionary position in his life. His sale was much more exciting. Loads of nude nymphs: we were very taken with a classic figure of a maiden, semi-clothed, carrying a pitcher, and also a statue of Leda and the swan. Lucky bird! But that turned out to be reconstituted stone too, so in the end we just bought a cast-iron boot scraper. Hiccup was actually right when he used to boast that the only thing worth pinching in the place was the girl groom's bottom.

Now we're home, we can start placing the pots. Veronica's

planting delphiniums to flower next year. Her tweed back-side looks rather good, echoing the yew archways. Grizel can cook us some lunch, then she can lug the pots around. We must position them exactly right. Vistas are what matter — lead the eye on. We all know that men are vile, but it's important that every prospect pleases.

A Hopeless Case

35

Guinevere decided that Grizel had better be smart-ened up for Bounder and Araminta's wedding, so she sent her to Jean-Marie in London.

Grizel's such a drip. Grace Atherstone nicknamed her 'the Auntie Depressant'. Flyaway hair and a flyaway husband, that was Grizel. Reggie left her because she wouldn't stop guest-feeding. There wasn't a homeless unemployed single parent or rescued black labrador cross she didn't ask to her grisly dinner parties.

Grizel was absolutely petrified. She hadn't been to a hairdresser since she was a girl. In fact, her hair died thirty years ago under an Alice band and a headscarf. She had risen at dawn to wash it, but still it drooped. Funny that the same style should look so ravishing on Phineas, her spaniel. But Phineas had a round face. Grizel had always had a long one.

Guinevere, Hortensia and all the Juggernaunts doted on Jean-Marie, a fat, bitchy old queen, with his *Finchley-en-Provence* accent and a tongue so sharp he hardly needed scissors.

Now he raises a strand with a pale pearl hand and smirks: 'Dear, dear, you wouldn't see a tail like this on a self-respecting rat.'

Grizel shrivels.

'Only joking, dear. How's Guin? She's a scream, Guin.'

Jean-Marie seems to know all Gervase's 'nephews': Caspar, Tristan, Ninian and Boris the Burglar, who was back from Morocco with a lovely tan.

'I gave him a sapphire rinse this morning, matching his eyes. He really is to dye for.'

The owner of the salon handles Jean-Marie with kid gloves, because if he stormed out he could take five hundred clients with him. It's normally eight weeks and holding even for a trim. If Guin hadn't phoned personally . . .

Everyone swears by Jean-Marie and Jean-Marie swears at everyone. Grizel gazes longingly at two Juggernaunts sailing by on their Knightsbridge legs for tea at Harrods and agrees to the whole works, she's *so* demoralised.

First her hair is wrapped in packets of foil till the ammonia makes her eyes water, then she's cut, coloured, conditioned and treated. Jean-Marie combs her out, his contempt drying and frizzing her hair in a trice.

As he brandishes the looking glass to reveal bleached locks, like droopy stubble in a cornfield, which in turn reveal bright red ears sticking out at right angles, Grizel remembers why she kept the same comfortingly concealing hairstyle for thirty years. Yet all she mutters is: 'Yes, wonderful, thank you.'

The bill uses up all her tiny allowance from Rufus for the next five years. If it weren't for Phineas, still looking at her with love, she'd jump under a taxi.

Dog Day Afternoon

36

Aunt Bridget goes to London.

Hell and damnation! I've been round Knightsbridge and the Cadogans twenty times trying to find a square foot of grass for Bertie to widdle on. It's all one-way and traffic wardens *everywhere*. I loathe London, particularly in August, when it's baking and crawling with ghastly tourists. Geddout of my way! That crossing's for zebras, stupid, not pedestrians!

Got to find a present for Araminta. Lists at the GTC and Good's indeed! Why can't she have it at Woolworth's. If she thinks I'm going to cough up for a Limoges dinner service, she's got another think coming. Oh God! Here's another thing coming shaking its fist. Damn cheek! How was I to know this was one-way? Never give men an inch. When Rollo was alive he stayed in his place behind the dog grid. And I've still got to find something to wear for the wedding. Rufus says I can't wear troos. Pompous ass. Pshaw!

Hell, here's Hans Crescent for the twenty-first time. Going to risk it and nip into Harrods. Get your paws on the wheel, Bertie, and drive round the block, if you see a traffic warden.

Here we are: first floor, nothing but coats and skirts in pastel colours. Show up every pawmark. Whaddjamean, dress it up with a beret and high heels? I'll beret you, my girl, and I haven't got out of gym shoes or gum boots for forty years.

Better try upstairs. What's this? The Way In? Sounds like another One-Way. Quite like that leather top-coat. Always wanted one. Here we are: changing rooms. Good God! Must have arrived in heaven. Far as the eye can see in misted-up spectacles, lovely girls stripped down to their knickers wriggling in and out of dresses. Steady on, Bridget! Good God, if it weren't for poor Bertie, stuck in the car . . .

Sugar! I'm about to be clamped. Whaddjamean, dog driving without a seat-belt?

A Rancorous Run-Up

37

Excitement was mounting at Flatgrove.

The wedding invitations had gone out. But only after the UN Peacekeeping Force had been moved in to defuse the hostilities. It was so confusing with four Countess Atherstones to be taken into account. Half the cousins were enraged because they hadn't been asked to the church. There simply wasn't room. Juggernaunts needed half a pew each and Rosebud, who seemed to be growing larger and larger, had got so fat that it was debatable if she'd even get up the aisle.

Knowing the young were incapable of answering invitations, Rufus had relented and allowed an 'I will/I will not be able to accept' postcard to be included in the envelope. But he flatly refused to let the service be videoed, or to allow any cameras in church. There'd be quite enough flashing with Aristotle Popitoutalot in the congregation.

Grace was livid about the video. She'd hired Merchant Ivory to make it. She was using the wedding to pay back all her *demi-mondaine* riff-raff.

'Your ghastly sisters will drink two bottles each and eat for twenty, so why shouldn't little me invite a few chums?' (About seven hundred.)

Rufus, who was finding it very disturbing seeing so much of his lovely third wife, only caved in when Grace threatened to flog her kiss-and-tell memoirs to the *Sun* on the week of the wedding and 'tell them how miniscule your winkle was'. Rufus promptly wrote a cheque for Grace's wedding outfit, which cost more than the entire wedding.

Meanwhile, every silkworm in the country was on standby to provide enough silk for Araminta's wedding dress. She was feeling a little down because she hadn't seen anything of Bounder since Ascot. He'd been so busy cub-hunting and playing polo. And she'd found herself looking after Hooligan, who'd been a bit of a liability. Suffering from withdrawal symptoms because of his master's absence and the start of the coursing season, from which he was now banned, he appeared to have emptied Lincolnshire of pheasants.

Then only last week he had eaten a brace of Flatgrove peacocks, and eviscerated a king-size duvet Araminta and Bounder had been given as a wedding present, which caused more feathers to fly than 12th August.

But at least on 27th September, Bounder would be back to marry her and bring Hooligan to heel. How lucky she was, thought Araminta. She loved him so much. His guest list was so dashingly showbiz, jet set and littered with exes. Gertie Grasping and her husband (who was rubbing his palms at the prospect of Araminta's dowry) were the only blots. The Atherstones also had to ask Piggy because he was a relation.

Only three days to go. Rufus was apoplectic. Half the young still hadn't filled in the 'I will/I will not' cards and Hooligan was in disgrace again. He had rushed out of the house that morning barking: 'Must have a peahen,' and he did.

Despite the recession, however, the wedding presents were wonderful. Rather to her bewilderment, Araminta had been sent fifty copies of *The Joy of Sex* by different guests. Only Grizel sent her a book extolling *The Joy of Celibacy*, because you never had to shut your eyes and think of Maastricht ever again.

Gaining a Son

38

ounder's parents, Josslyn and Sybil, were due to arrive any minute from San Francisco. Rosebud was deeply moved when Bounder insisted they'd want to share a bedroom. How romantic after thirty-five years together!

Josslyn and Sybil were not quite what the Atherstones had expected. They rolled up in Josslyn's Lagonda, which had been flown over specially. Josslyn, who kept the spare tyres round her waist, had been seriously wild in her youth, roaring round San Francisco on a Harley-Davidson as a founder member of the notorious Dykes-on-Bykes Brigade. She'd also marched in Gay Parades, yelling: 'Two four six eight, how d'ya know your grandma's straight!'

In middle age, however, she had settled down and become famous as an atonal composer. She had just recorded her first opera, a sequel to *William Tell* called *Kissund Tell*, only this time, the arrow went straight through Little Kissund's jugular rather than the apple. During the *entr'acte* there was a ballet of telephone-tap-dancing.

Rosebud and Araminta thought Sybil was dreadfully creepy, like the wicked fairy putting a curse on the wedding. She was so rouged and painted, she'd crumble to nothing if you removed her make-up. Caliban used to dig pignuts with his long nails. Sybil didn't look as though she'd dig anything – except gold. Hooligan's hackles wouldn't go down. How could those two be Bounder's parents?

Over drinks before dinner, Josslyn and Sybil revealed they had adopted Bounder, whose real name was Bernard, when he was a few hours old.

'Never liked children,' admitted Josslyn, knocking her pipe out against the chimney-piece. 'But Sybil, who was briefly in PR, had a big diaper account and wanted some practice.'

'But who was Bounder's – I mean Bernard's – father?' asked Rufus, aghast.

'Played polo for the Argentine,' boomed Jossyln. 'Never met the mother, believe she was married. Terrified her husband might come back from abroad, realise the kid wasn't his.'

Rufus actually thought Josslyn was quite a sound fellow. Reminded him of his Aunt Rosemary, who wanted to be one of her four brothers and always wore corduroy trousers, a hairnet and four Huskies, one on top of the other. Josslyn had brought him four crates of Californian wine, which Drinkwater mercifully hadn't got his hands on yet, and some excellent cigars, which was more than Piggy Atherstone had ever done. He was completely won over, after the ladies had left the dining-room, when Josslyn titillated him with stories of Madonna, with whom she'd actually worked.

Aunt Pansy, however, who was invited over for coffee to meet Josslyn and Sybil, and who had been presented with a signed copy of *Kissund Tell* for her 'Seedy Walker', was seriously alarmed. Bounder was a sweet boy. How awful for him to have been brought up by two Elizabethans.

Araminta, too, was utterly distraught. She didn't know which one to treat as her mother-in-law, Sybil or Josslyn. How gross for poor darling Bounder to have parents like that!

But all this was forgotten when Rosebud started groaning and clutching her monstrous belly. Inconvenient if the old girl were ill before the wedding, thought Rufus, although it would make more room for everyone else. Fortunately, Josslyn, who had had long experience of breeding bull mastiffs, knew exactly what was happening and whisked Rosebud into Lincoln hospital in her Lagonda. And at seven the following morning, Rosebud, Countess of Atherstone, gave birth to a twelve-pound boy. Rufus was gobsmacked. He couldn't imagine anyone fancying Rosebud.

'It's yours, Juggins,' whispered an exhausted but overjoyed Rosebud. 'Don't you remember Boxing Night?'

At first, Rufus only remembered the Madonna book. 'So was it *your* bedroom I ended up in?' he asked in amazement.

And suddenly he was like a very old dog with twenty-two tails because he had a tiny heir to inherit the title and everything else. Blood was much thicker than water purifiers, and now dreadful Piggy would be out on his silk purse.

Initially, Piggy was tempted to slit his throat. Then he chortled. With the birth of little Rufus and the law of primogeniture, Araminta would be hardly worth a bean. There was no way Bounder would stand by a penniless somebody. Serve her right, thought Piggy, waddling off to find a telephone box he could fit into, to ring the *Sun*.

Word instantly got round that Bounder was on the market again. The flag was raised at Annabel's; San Lorenzo emerged from its vale of tears and there was dancing in the streets of Kensington and Knightsbridge. But poor Araminta hung down her head and cried, and Lightning raised her head and howled.

Josslyn, on the other hand, didn't appreciate the significance of these events. Humming the twelve-tone room-bugging theme from *Kissund Tell* and wanting a butchers at the legendarily beautiful Grace Atherstone who was due for lunch, she drove back to Flatgrove from the hospital. She also remembered that she and Sybil had promised to reveal to Bounder the identity of his father the day before his wedding. So while everyone was drinking the health of Rufus's new heir, she handed her adopted son a photograph of a tall, dark man even handsomer than himself.

'Good God!' exploded Rufus, peering over Bounder's shoulder. 'That chap used to play for me.'

'Good God,' said Grace faintly. 'That man used to play *with* me.'

She was just telling everyone that the man in the photograph was Horacio, Rufus's one-time Argentinian polo player, when Aunt Pansy fainted.

'Give her some air,' shouted Bounder, who'd always had a soft spot for Pansy and, picking her up, he laid her gently on the sofa. As there were no smelling salts, he mopped her brow with an emerald-green handkerchief smelling faintly of Penhaligon's 'Bluebell.'

'Give her some air,' he repeated, shoving Josslyn aside.

'I think she's given me an heir,' whispered Aunt Pansy. 'When is your birthday, Bernard?'

'February 1st,' said Bounder.

'Then you *are* my heir,' cried Pansy. 'The smell of blue-bells brought it all back. When I was painting in the life class last spring, I knew I'd seen one of those things before. now I've remembered where: it was in Flatgrove Clump during bluebell time. On the end of it was an Argentine polo player called Horacio. He was so dashing. I was married, but for a few glorious moments, I forgot myself. The result, little Bernard, was you. Hector, my husband, was exploring the Antarctic at the time. We had a *mariage blanc*, so he'd have known he couldn't possibly be the father. I was so terrified of scandal, I gave you up for absorption.'

Aunt Pansy had to borrow Bounder's handkerchief again. 'Too late, I learned that Hector had been eaten by a polar bear, so I could have kept you,' she sobbed. 'There hasn't been a single day since that I haven't regretted it.'

'Look, look.' With trembling fingers, Pansy managed to open the locket round her neck to show a crumpled photograph of the tiniest scrap of humanity. 'And it grew into this beautiful young man, oh Bernard, Bernard!' Pansy opened her arms.

'Oh, Mummy, Mummy,' cried Bounder joyfully. Sybil had always insisted he call her Sybil. 'If I'd invented a mother, you would have been she.'

So overnight Bounder found himself worth millions and the poor National Canine Defence League was suddenly feeling very undefended.

'Ha, ha, ha,' chortled Piggy, as he waddled off to give another instalment to the *Sun*. 'He's even less likely to marry Minta now he's going to be one of the richest men in England.'

But at that moment, Bounder gazed out of the window and saw a mighty protest march of his exes, most of whom had slept with him as a wedding present, storming up the drive, brandishing 'Bounder Belongs To Me' placards. The march spread back across the flat Lincolnshire countryside as far as the eye could see, probably all the way back to Belgrave Square and the Cadogans. An army ready to nail him, now he was rich and free.

Suddenly, he decided he would do anything for a quiet wife.

'Would you like me to marry Araminta?' he asked his new mother.

'She is my favourite niece,' cried Aunt Pansy. 'It would make me die happy.'

'And fairly quickly, perhaps,' murmured Bounder, thinking of his debts.

So he wiped away Araminta's tears with a still-dry corner of the bluebell-scented silk handkerchief.

'Of course the wedding will go on, my angel.'

And it did.

The Gossips

39

Everyone in London was electrified by the goings-on at Flatgrove. Cousins Flavia and Cedric blissfully inhaled puffs of smoke and gossip.

'My dear, the rush to the newspapers has been positively Gadarene. Grace, Boris, Drinkwater and Piggy all trying to flog their stories, with Flappy Foxe-Whapshott frantically trying to stop them. Boris got there first. It was in the *Sun* this morning:

EARL'S SISTER IN ARGY LOVE-CHILD TANGLE
"My brother Rufus is on stand-by," claims Lady Pansy.
"My proudest moment," says New Dad Earl.

Flappy's furious, of course, because Baby Rufus is positive proof that Rufus Père had been cheating on her with his *own* wife. I mean, Rufus was always the one who kissed and Flappy turned the cheek in that relationship. And now the old bat is finding it frite-fly difficult to turn the *other* cheek and forgive Rufus.'

'And poor Minta's got so thin belting away from her future mother-in-law, she's down to size sixteen and still shrinking. The wedding dress has been taken in twice.'

'Shall we have another bottle?'

'Why not? Ring the bell, would you? How's Gervase?'

'Terrible. He's had to move to Barnes. He'll never survive the humiliation of an 081 telephone number.'

'Poor fellow!'

'But he's such a bitch, Ceedy. He gave a surprise forty-fifth birthday party for Grace at the Ivy the other night, which was a particularly horrific surprise for her, because she's sworn to everyone, including Nigel Dempster, that she's only thirty-four. *Anyway,* it was an even more horrific surprise for the rest of us, because we were expected to pay for our own dinner. Grace got her own back on Gervase, however, by annexing Boris the Burglar. She always liked her peasants well hung.'

Bring Back Hanging on Every Word

40

Effie's sister, Minkie, is such a scream. Her friends are enraptured. The tiny dog listens in amazement. Even the waiter is rooted to the spot, horrified yet too fascinated to tear himself away.

'Darlings, darlings, the wedding's on again. I cannot believe Bounder's ability to bound back. There he was – the debtor's prison looming and next moment Pansy's made everything over to him to avoid capital transfer, all except half a million to the NCDL.'

'Lucky Minta getting Bounder and all that money.'

'Bounder'll never be faithful to her.'

'Never, never, but she'll have her dogs and her garden and Pansy's coming to live with them, so she won't be lonely. And talking of pansies, you'll never guess what.'

'Go on.' Minkie's friends wiggle their feet in excitement.

'Gervase went out to Gays last night to drown his sorrows after Boris chucked him, and thought he saw a centipede swimming round in his bowl of soup. Looking down, he realised it was a false eyelash belonging to the utterly ravishing waiter who was serving him, so Gervase invited him home.'

'All the way to Barnes, that *is* a test of true love.'

'And Ramon-Octavio — that's his name, can you *believe* it — went. And now they're an item. And they're going to spend their wedding night in the bridal suite of the Oscar Wilde Hotel in Oxford and miss Minta's wedding.'

'And so will Piggy. Rufus has banned him because he tried to sell a story about Rosebud having a virgin birth to the *Sunday Sport*, so he could inherit the title after all. Gosh, I'm going to enjoy this wedding!'

Brightly Dawned Their Wedding Day

41

Everyone was back from their holidays, so the church at Flatgrove was absolutely packed. The service was enlivened by a punch-up between Gertie Grasping and an usher because Aunt Pansy, as one of the bridegroom's three mothers, had taken the last seat in the front pew.

The music was also a bit of a shock. Out went the 'Wedding March', 'Here Comes the Bride', 'Praise my Soul' and

'*Panis Angelicus*'. In came atonal hymns composed by Josslyn, punctuated by traditional sobs from the bride's mother, because her frumpy daughter was marrying one of the most eligible men in England.

Coming up the aisle to the '*Exposé*' theme from *Kissund Tell*, Araminta nervously clutched her white roses and stephanotis like a child holding a torch in the dark. She was so shattered by the experience of arranging the entire wedding that when the parson asked her whether she, Araminta Grace Pansy Hope Dymphna, would take this man to be her lawful wedded husband, she mindlessly answered: 'I will stroke will not be able to accept your invitation for September the twenty-seventh, delete as applicable.'

Having given away his daughter, Rufus collapsed into the pew beside Rosebud for a good sleep.

'For richer for pawer,' whispered Hooligan, giving Lightning a lick. Everyone agreed that they'd never seen dogs more in love, and that Minta and Bounder would stay together because of the lurchers.

When Bounder and Araminta went up the aisle for the parson's pep talk, the choir sang the 'Confrontation Aria' from *Kissund Tell*: 'His wife is standing by him'.

Waking with a start, expecting '*Panis Angelicus*' and the enjoyment of a good blub, Rufus started to sing along and had his ears boxed by Josslyn.

'No commentio

Best friend of the Wifeo . . .'
sang the choir.

Hat Attack

42

Grace Atherstone had never looked more beautiful in her new black suit, which would double up for memorial services – after Alcoholics Anonymous meetings, they were the best pick-up places these days.

She wasn't into toe-sucking. Pate-tickling was far more fun. Grace tickled Percy Ponsonby-Porter so much in church, he burst into high-pitched giggles and begged for mercy.

'The balder, the more beautiful,' whispered Grace, batting her eyelashes.

'Didyer know Baldor the Beautiful had a mother called Frigg?' demanded Josslyn, who'd taken a shine to Grace.

But Grace didn't want Sybil getting jealous and putting a hex on her, so she concentrated on Percy.

'Do you like my hat?' she asked.

'I like what's under it better,' admitted Percy.

Silly old wimp, thought Grace, who only liked unadulterated praise, and decided to go back to Boris the Burglar, who was much more fun. Having broken into all the best houses in England, he had had no problem crashing the wedding.

Mistaken Identical

43

*S*trordinary how some men go for the same type.

Tanya and Pamela, two of Bounder's exes, had thought and thought and thought about what they could wear to make Bounder stop in his tracks halfway up the aisle, or at least bitterly regret what he was chucking away. So they each went off and spent a fortune on a distinctive and — they each thought — utterly unique outfit. The moral is, never go to a top designer for a special occasion.

Pamela had picked out the gold in the coat. Tanya had picked out the green with matching bag and green tinted stockings. But they still looked the same.

'Ghastly tarty earrings,' hissed Pamela.

'Even tartier to have a ghastly ring outside one's glove,' hissed Tanya.

Aunt Pansy made everything much worse by enquiring if Tanya and Pamela were identical twins.

It was definitely hatpins at dawn.

The Ride of the Vel-Crows

44

ousin Carabosse wrote books. She had made an absolute bomb from *The Belly and Bosom Diet Book*. She was a third cousin of Rufus's, not nearly far enough removed. Brought up in Hong Kong, Carabosse said: 'Chin, chin; chin, chin,' every time she took a slug of what should have been Krug, if Drinkwater hadn't drunk it all.

Carabosse was a man-eater. She had already eaten the

best man and a busload of tenants from Wales. And, what with the new leasehold law reform, Rufus was having trouble with his tenants in Lincolnshire, so Carabosse was about to gobble them up too.

Hooligan Longtail had designs on Carabosse's Valkyrie hat, but as he edged up he realised she had designs on him too.

'Excuse me, I've just seen a superfluous hare,' woofed Hooligan, escaping out of the window.

Meanwhile Faith and Hope were wishing they had a bag like Carabosse's for pinching cuttings, and Grace Atherstone was taking Boris on a tour of her old home. She was pointing out her own portrait next to the Titian Madonna, radiant in the afternoon sunshine.

Come Fly with Me

45

Rufus heaved a sigh of relief. Bounder and Araminta were going away at last. He had never known people drink so much champagne – even more than Drinkwater. As Araminta, in her bright red going-away suit, chucked her bouquet down the great Flatgrove stairway, the ravening horde of Bounder's exes ripped it apart like Actaeon.

Flatgrove had never looked more lovely than in the falling

September sunshine with the trees just turning and lime keys all over the lawns. Some of the dogs were wearing bows to wave goodbye to Hooligan and Lightning. The helicopter blades were lifting hats and dresses. That's the nearest Araminta's going to get to a chopper this weekend, thought Bounder's exes sourly. Even worse, Carabosse seemed to have eaten all the spare men.

Everyone waved, as if at a rock concert. Aunt Pansy wiped her eyes. So lovely to see her darling boy so happily settled: 'God bless you. Good luck. Send us a postcard.'

With marriage today, it's like launching a little boat on a stormy sea, all one can do is pray.

While everyone was so diverted, Boris and Grace and the Titian Madonna took the opportunity to steal away into the sunset, towards the car park. Serve Rufus right for being stingy with alimony, thought Grace. She and Boris would have to have their faces completely redone if they ever wanted to come back to England.

'Don't forget the clocks go back tonight,' she reminded Aristotle Popitoutalot on the way out.

The honeymoon was spent in Ireland, so that Bounder could carry on cub-hunting and the dogs could come too. They were all staying in one of Pansy's spare towers, which turned out to be a lovely little castle in Wicklow.

Bounder felt very happy. The only strings attached now would be those of polo ponies. He thought he and Araminta would do very well, now she'd lost so much weight. There was no way he was going to forsake all others, but he might cut down a bit. Whistling to Hooligan, who was suffering from indigestion, having eaten both Carabosse's hat and Boris's car keys, Bounder went out to stretch his legs and ring Effie from the telephone box in the village.

Trying not to feel homesick, Araminta snuggled down in the huge carved four-poster. She felt comforted as she remembered her mother's pre-wedding pep talk the night before, when Grace had quoted from *Locksley Hall*:

> *He will hold thee, when his passion shall have spent*
> *its novel force,*
> *Something better than his dog, a little dearer than his*
> *horse.*

'But that's wonderful,' Araminta had said in a choked voice. 'Imagine the bliss of being loved even more than Hooligan and Bounder's polo ponies.'

She'd always known that men marry for rank, land and money and get their fun elsewhere, as her father had done. Bounder had already bought a house in the Boltons and a country cottage where he could join her and Pansy sometimes at weekends. It had a dear little garden which had been neglected and at least there'd be more hound puppies to walk when she got home. But she hoped that, after that awful childhood, she could make Bounder happy. She loved him so much. She touched wood.

Beside her, Lightning Longtail (née Atherstone), who still had stephanotis petals in her shaggy brown fur, stretched out her paws and in her sleep touched one of the carved wooden bedposts.